Hello, Family Members,

Learning to read is one of the most important accomplishments of early childhood. **Hello Reader!** books are designed to help children become skilled readers who like to read. Beginning readers learn to read by remembering frequently used words like "the," "is," and "and"; by using phonics skills to decode new words; and by interpreting picture and text clues. These books provide both the stories children enjoy and the structure they need to read fluently and independently. Here are suggestions for helping your child *before*, *during*, and *after* reading:

Before
- Look at the cover and pictures and have your child predict what the story is about.
- Read the story to your child.
- Encourage your child to chime in with familiar words and phrases.
- Echo read with your child by reading a line first and having your child read it after you do.

During
- Have your child think about a word he or she does not recognize right away. Provide hints such as "Let's see if we know the sounds" and "Have we read other words like this one?"
- Encourage your child to use phonics skills to sound out new words.
- Provide the word for your child when more assistance is needed so that he or she does not struggle and the experience of reading with you is a positive one.
- Encourage your child to have fun by reading with a lot of expression . . . like an actor!

After
- Have your child keep lists of interesting and favorite words.
- Encourage your child to read the books over and over again. Have him or her read to brothers, sisters, grandparents, and even teddy bears. Repeated readings develop confidence in young readers.
- Talk about the stories. Ask and answer questions. Share ideas about the funniest and most interesting characters and events in the stories.

I do hope that you and your child enjoy this book.

—Francie Alexander
Reading Specialist,
Scholastic's Learning Ventures

To dolphins, with love
—F.M.

In memory of my dad
—L.S.

Special thanks to Laurie Roulston
of the Denver Museum of
Natural History for her expertise

Text copyright © 1999 by Faith McNulty.
Illustrations copyright © 1999 by Lena Shiffman.
All rights reserved. Published by Scholastic Inc.
SCHOLASTIC, HELLO READER!, CARTWHEEL BOOKS and associated logos
are trademarks and/or registered trademarks of Scholastic Inc.

Library of Congress Cataloging-in-Publication Data

McNulty, Faith.
    Playing with dolphins / by Faith McNulty; illustrated by Lena Shiffman.
       p.   cm.— (Hello reader! Science. Level 4)
    Summary: While visiting her sister who is studying dolphins in Florida, a young girl has an exciting day swimming in the dolphin pool, watching a pregnant dolphin give birth, and finally, having her life saved by one of the animals.
    ISBN 0-590-63606-5
    1.Dolphins—Juvenile fiction. [1. Dolphins—Fiction.]
I. Shiffman, Lena, ill. II. Title. III. Series.
PZ7.M24P1   1999
[E]—dc21   98-34756
                                                    CIP
                                                      AC

12 11 10 9 8 7 6 5 4 3 2 1   9/9 0/0 01 02 03 04
Printed in the U.S.A.   24
First printing, April 1999

Playing With
Dolphins

by Faith McNulty
Illustrated by Lena Shiffman

Hello Reader! Science — Level 4

SCHOLASTIC INC.
New York Toronto London Auckland Sydney

This is the story of a day
I'll never forget —
when I swam with dolphins
and saw a baby dolphin born.

My older sister, Beth, had a job at
an aquarium in Florida.
Dolphins were kept there
for scientists to study.
She invited me to visit her
and learn about dolphins.

"Bring your mask and flippers," she said.
"We'll swim with the dolphins."

Beth met me at the airport and we drove
to the shore of the bay.
We sat on a dock at the
water's edge.
Beth pointed to a line of buoys
marking an underwater fence.
She explained that the fence kept the dolphins
from swimming away to the open water.

Then she put her hand in the
water and splashed.
"That's a way to call them," she said.
Suddenly, a long, gray form
flashed through the water, and
a dolphin popped up beside us.

"Hi, Amelia," Beth said,
smiling down at the dolphin.
"How are you? I'm so glad to see you!"

The dolphin bobbed in the water and
regarded us with shiny, dark eyes.
Her curved mouth opened and
I heard a creaking sound,
like a rusty hinge.
I wondered if she was saying,
"Fine, thanks! How are you?"

"She's my favorite," Beth said.
"She's expecting a baby.
It could happen any day."

Beth reached down and stroked
the rounded top of Amelia's head.
"They love to be stroked," she said,
"and to be talked to."

She reached into a bucket
and held out a small fish.
Rising almost upright, Amelia opened
her mouth and took it from Beth's fingers.

I saw Amelia's row of teeth and wondered
if she might bite someone —
even by mistake.

Beth handed me a fish.
When I hesitated, she said,
"It's okay. She knows how to do it."

I held out the fish by the tail.
Amelia rose and took it gently,
without even touching my fingers.

"You can pat her on the head," Beth said,
"but don't touch her blowhole."

I could see a hole at the top of her head,
open and close, open and close,
as she bobbed up and down in the water.
"That's how she breathes," Beth
explained. "You wouldn't want a hand
over your nose."

In spite of a few butterflies in my stomach,
I reached down and gently touched Amelia.
Her skin was satin smooth.
I had never seen a live dolphin before.
Now I had touched one!
That was exciting enough.
I had no way of knowing that very soon
a dolphin would save my life.

Beth picked up the bucket.
"That's all for now. I have work to do.
Goodbye, Amelia."
She turned away.
Amelia dove and vanished.

Beth's morning chores began with
fixing meals of fish and vitamins
    for each of the seven dolphins
        at the aquarium.
            We talked while she worked.

Beth told me that dolphins are descended
from land animals that went into the sea
millions of years ago.
Little by little, these animals changed their
shape to suit their new way of life.

Inside, dolphins are still very much
like land animals.
They breathe air. Their blood is warm.
They feed their young with milk.

Dolphins are found in the sea
wherever the water is warm
and there are fish to be caught.

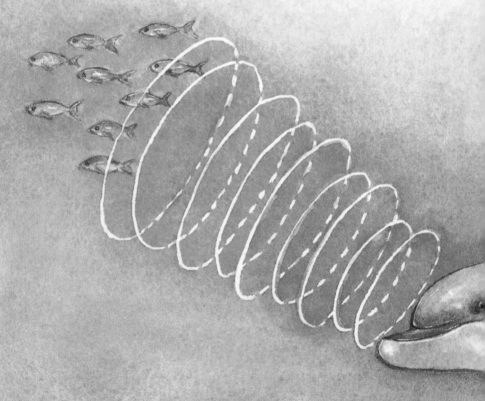

Their lives were mysterious
until we began to study
tame dolphins like Amelia.
What we have learned is amazing.

Dolphins use their eyes in daylight,
but have a special way of "seeing"
in the darkness underwater.
They make clicking sounds
that travel through the water.
When the sound waves hit
something solid, they bounce back.
The returning sound wave
tells the dolphin what's ahead.
This way of "seeing in the dark"
is called "echolocation."

Like many land animals, including humans,
dolphins live together in groups.
All of the dolphins in the group
depend on each other.
If one dolphin is hurt or in danger,
the others try to rescue it.
They will lift a drowning dolphin
to the surface so it can breathe.

Dolphins "talk" with whistling sounds.
(Of course, nobody knows
what they are saying.)

Families of mothers and their young
are especially close.
They often touch and stroke each other.
Young dolphins chase and play.
A dolphin separated from the group
is frightened and miserable.

"This need to be together is
probably the reason wild dolphins
can be tamed," Beth said.
"Because they trust each other,
they can learn to trust the humans
who care for them."

Beth finished her chores.
"Now," she said, "it's time to check on
Amelia and see how that baby is coming.
A baby dolphin stays inside the mother for
a long time before it is born."

Beth explained that Amelia had mated
with one of the males in the group
almost a year before.

Now she showed signs that birth was near.
One sign was a change in her behavior.
She stayed away from the group
and close to her friend Annie.

When a dolphin gives birth, another female
often stays with her, ready to help.
Annie would be Amelia's helper,
and would be like an aunt to the baby
when it was born.

Beth stood at the edge of the dolphin
pool and blew a whistle.
"Dolphins are taught that a whistle
means food," Beth said.
A moment later, a dark fin cut through
the water and Amelia arrived at the dock.
She watched as Beth
took a fish from a bucket.
Bobbing in the water, Amelia
reminded me of a dog sitting up to beg.

Beth gave her the fish, then slid off
the dock and into the water beside her.

"Come on in," Beth called to me.
"It's perfectly safe. But remember that
dolphins are big, strong animals.
You can't play with them
as though they were puppies."

I put on my mask and slipped
into the cold, salty water.

I sank down and opened my eyes.
There was Amelia, swimming close to me.
She looked huge.
She glided through the water,
circling around me as though
she were checking me out.

I hope she will like me,
I thought. *How do I tell her*
I want to be friends?
I came up to breathe.

Suddenly, I felt something hard and slippery
touch my leg and I almost screamed.
Amelia surged past me,
making the water swirl.

"Don't be scared," Beth called.
"She just wants to know you."
Beth slapped the water,
and Amelia came to her.
Beth put her hand flat on the water.
Amelia swam slowly under it,
rubbing her back against Beth's palm.

"Put out your hand," Beth said.
"That means you're offering to rub her back."
I put out my hand.
Amelia pressed against it.
As she glided past, I could feel the power of
her hard, smooth body under my hand.

"Here's something else she likes,"
Beth said. "We play copy cat."
She turned on her side and waved
one arm in the air.
Amelia did likewise, waving one flipper.

"Your turn," Beth said.
"Do something she can copy."
I began to whirl around like a top.

A moment later, Amelia, head out of water,
was whirling, too.

Then Beth began jumping up and down.
Amelia did the same.
Beth was laughing and
Amelia looked as though
she were laughing, too.

"Would you like a fast ride?"
Beth asked.
"Lie on your back."
I lay on my back, staring into the blue sky.
I felt Amelia beside me.
"Now grab her fin,"
Beth called, "and
hang on."

I grabbed Amelia's fin and she took off
like a racehorse, dragging me head first.
As we surged through the water
in dizzy circles, all I could see
was foam and sky.
Totally in her power, I felt like a toy.

Suddenly she halted and I let go.
"Did you like it?" Beth asked.
I said, "Terrific!" and meant it.

"Now," Beth said, "it's time for
Amelia's checkup."
She told me to get some fish from
the dock, while she led Amelia into
shallow water.

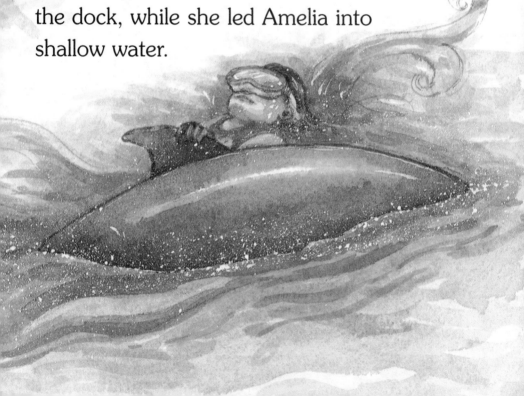

Beth wanted to measure Amelia
around the middle to see if
her belly was getting bigger.
This was something Amelia didn't like.
She wiggled and squirmed.
When Beth got the tape around her,
Amelia slipped away.
Beth went on trying, but I could see
she was losing patience.

Finally Beth straightened up.
"Okay, Amelia," she said.
"I'm leaving!"

Beth climbed onto the dock
and stood there stiffly
with her back turned to the water.

Amelia bobbed up and down in the water.
She made sounds as though
she were calling Beth back.

"She knows I'm mad at her," Beth
explained. "If you threaten to go away,
dolphins usually behave."

A few minutes later,
Beth turned around and
went back in the water with Amelia.
This time Amelia held still.

"Now let's see your tummy," Beth said.
At the word "tummy," Amelia rolled over.
Beth was smiling as she examined her.
"Hey, that's great!" she said.
"I think she's making milk!"

"She might have the baby tonight,"
Beth said, as we climbed out of the pool.
"But I hope it's tomorrow.
I want to be here in case
anything goes wrong."

"What could go wrong?" I asked.
"Usually nothing," Beth said.
"Dolphins give birth quite easily.
But sometimes the baby
needs help. It has to get to
the surface quickly or it will
drown."

***

Early the next morning,
Beth and I were at the pool.
She called Amelia to breakfast,
but the dolphin didn't appear.
As we scanned the water, two dolphins
surfaced at the far end of the pool.
"That must be Amelia and Annie,"
Beth said. "Let's go have a look."

We swam out to the far corner
of the pool where the dolphins had been,
but they were not in sight.
Swimming underwater we searched until
we ran out of breath.

Still no luck.
Then Beth noticed that a number
of plastic bags were stuck
in the mesh of the fence.

"This stuff is deadly to dolphins," Beth said.
"They can swallow it by mistake."
I helped her clear the bags away and
roll them into a ball to carry to the dock.

Beth started back with the trash.
Instead of following her, I swam
along the fence line.
I loved looking down through my mask
at the landscape of white sand, and into the
soft blue-green water ahead.

Suddenly, I saw two dolphins
swimming near the surface.
Amelia and Annie!
I recognized Amelia by her darker color.
She was behaving strangely,
twisting and turning in the water.
She arched her back and then bent forward,
like a person reaching for his toes.

Annie was close by.
Now and then she touched
Amelia with her nose,
or rubbed her with a flipper.

I watched as they swam
in big circles.
They didn't seem to notice me at all.
Suddenly I saw a dark shape emerging
from the underside of Amelia's belly.
Her baby was being born!
In a few seconds, the newborn dolphin
was free.
Amelia gently pushed the baby to the surface.
Annie was beside her, helping.

I raised my head out of the water
to call Beth.
She was near the dock,
swimming slowly in my direction.
I yelled for her to hurry.
When she didn't seem to hear,
I yelled again.

Treading water and waving to Beth,
I took a deep breath for another yell.
Suddenly I breathed in water.
I choked and gasped.
I remember the feeling of panic as I
struggled for air.
Forgetting how to swim, I thrashed
in the water.
I sank under the surface.
That was the moment that a dolphin
saved my life.
I felt its powerful body beneath me,
pushing and shoving me upward.
My head was above the water!
I could breathe!

Too exhausted to swim, I lay on
the dolphin's back, hanging onto her fin.
Beth arrived.
She took me in a lifeguard's grip and
towed me to the dock.
She helped me up and sat beside me,
rubbing my shivering body with a towel.
For a moment, we were too breathless
to speak.

Then Beth gave a shout.
"Hey! Look! There it is!" she cried.
I sat up.
Beth was pointing at the water, where
Amelia and Annie were circling the dock
with a very small dolphin swimming
between them.
"It's born!" Beth cried. "That's wonderful!"

"I know," I said. "I saw it happen!"
Then I told her how I almost drowned and
a dolphin had held me up in the water.

"That must have been Annie," Beth said,
"doing her job. The mother and baby didn't
need her so she saved you instead."

Suddenly, I was so filled with gladness at being alive that I hugged Beth.

I wanted to hug Annie, too, but that wasn't possible, so I said in my heart, *Thank you, Annie, for saving my life.*